Alba – Book 5

A Bit

Reading Practice

ck	ng	qu	le
sock	sing	quit	giggle
pick	long	quack	apple
deck	hang	quill	juggle
rack	rung	quest	bottle
stuck	bring	quick	saddle
flick	stung		
block	slang		
pluck	strong		
track	string		

		wh	ed
		when	jumped
		which	dropped
		whip	sobbed
		what	grunted
		why	lifted

Contents

Vocabulary:

tumbled   – rolled end over end, as when falling

crumpled   – wrinkled or crushed

clung   – held tightly

fumbling   – feeling about clumsily

slung   – threw something

glum   – sad and gloomy

slotted   – fitted into a place or slot

mumbled   – spoke very quietly, hard to hear

Chapter 1
On the Bus

The bus rocked as it set off. Alba tripped and fell. She tumbled to the back of the bus.

A lot of things rolled along the bus.
A plastic bottle banged into Alba.
Crumpled bus tickets hit her leg.

A sock fell from a bag. Alba clung to it. It was thick and soft, but it did not stop her rattling along the bus.

Chapter 2
A Lost Ring

Alba spotted Todd in the bus. He was fumbling in his jacket pocket. "It's lost!" he yelled, as he held up a ring box.

Alba had spotted a ring rolling along the bus! She ran back to fetch it. It had got stuck in a crack.

The ring was stuck, but it shifted when Alba tugged at it. She picked it up and slung it on her back.

Chapter 3
String

Todd was glum. He sat with his chin in his hand. A long string hung from his jacket pocket.

Quick as a flash, Alba grabbed hold of the end of the string. It held strong when she tugged it. She swung on the end.

The string was thick and strong in Alba's hands. She dragged herself up it. With a quick flick of her legs, she swung herself onto Todd's lap.

Todd was fed up. The ring was for his mom and he had lost it. He did not spot Alba as she slotted the ring back in the box.

Chapter 4
As Soft as a Nest

"This pocket is the best spot to rest until the bus stops," Alba mumbled. The jacket pocket was as soft as a nest when she hopped into it.

Todd spotted the ring in the ring box. He grinned and began to sing. Snug in his pocket, Alba hummed along to his song.